M and M and The Big Bag

M & M and The Big Bag

by Pat Ross • pictures by Marylin Hafner

PUFFIN BOOKS

PUFFIN BOOKS
Published by the Penguin Group
Viking Penguin Inc., 40 West 23rd Street, New York, New York 10010, U.S.A.
Penguin Books Ltd, 27 Wrights Lane, London W8 5TZ England
Penguin Books Australia Ltd, Ringwood, Victoria, Australia
Penguin Books Canada Ltd, 2801 John Street, Markham, Ontario, Canada L3R 1B4
Penguin Books (N.Z.) Ltd, 182-190 Wairau Road, Auckland 10, New Zealand

Penguin Books Ltd, Registered Offices: Harmondsworth, Middlesex, England

First published by Pantheon Books 1981
Published in Picture Puffins 1985
Reprinted 1987

Library of Congress Cataloging in Publication Data
Ross, Pat. M and M and the big bag.
Summary: New at reading, Mandy and Mimi make their
first trip to the grocery store alone, proudly
carrying their grocery list.
1. Children's stories, American. [1. Shopping—
Fiction] I. Hafner, Marylin, ill. II. Title.
PZ7.R71973Mac 1985 [E] 84-16565 ISBN 0-14-031852-6 (pbk.)

Printed in U.S.A.
by R.R. Donnelley & Sons Company, Harrisonburg, Virginia
Set in Century Schoolbook

For Erica
and for her friend Gaelen
P.R.
To Katherine
M.H.

CHAPTER ONE

Mandy and Mimi—
the two friends
who called themselves M and M—
looked carefully
at the yellow sheet of paper.
The big black letters at the top
spelled GROCERY LIST.
But it was not
just *any* grocery list.
It was a very important grocery list.
So they read it three times.

Mandy and Mimi
were going to the grocery store
without a grown-up
for the very first time.
And the list was for them.
"This is it!" cried Mandy.
"It's about time!" cried Mimi.

The friends M and M
were ready for this day.
They could read prices and signs.
They could even read tricky words
like *cucumber* and *pizza*.

They could count their change.
And they always looked both ways
before they crossed the street.
They were ready all right—
ready to shop at The Big Bag alone.
They looked at the grocery list again.
The paper was clean and smooth.
The words were big and neat.
They read the list one more time—

GROCERY LIST

1 butter
1 bread
2 apples
1 box trash bags
1 milk

"That's an easy list," said Mimi.
"Nothing to it," said Mandy.

Mandy was in charge of the list.
She folded the paper
and tucked it under her belt.
Mimi was in charge of the money.
She pushed a five dollar bill
deep into her back pocket.
Then she wiggled and jumped
to make sure the money was safe.

"OK, let's move it!" Mimi shouted.
Mimi's dog Maxi ran to the door
and barked.
Maxi didn't want to be left behind.
"No Maxi," they said.
"You can't come."
But Maxi sat right by the door.

“OK, OK,” said Mimi.
“You win.
But you’d better be good.
We’re going to The Big Bag!”

CHAPTER TWO

Mandy and Mimi

had to cross two streets

to get to The Big Bag.

One street was big and wide.

It had noisy buses and fast cars.

M and M waited

for the green light

and the WALK sign

before they crossed the street.

The Big Bag had two front doors.
One said OUT
and NO BARE FEET.

The other said IN and

NO DOGS ALLOWED.

"That means you," said Mimi to Maxi.

Maxi didn't like being left outside—
not one bit!
He started to bark.
"Be a good dog!" said Mandy,
and she bent down to pat him.
Just then, a piece of paper—
a piece of yellow paper—
fell on the sidewalk.

Mandy didn't see it fall.
Mimi didn't see it fall.
But Maxi did.
Maxi barked at the paper.
"Come on," said Mimi.
"Maxi always makes a fuss.
Just pretend you don't know him."
So M and M turned away
and they went into The Big Bag.

CHAPTER THREE

"What's first on the list?" asked Mimi.

Mandy reached under her belt.

"It's gone!" she cried.

"What are we going to do?"

"Who needs that list anyway?
We know what to buy," said Mimi.

“Are you sure?” asked Mandy.

She wished they had the list.

“Yes, I’m sure,” said Mimi.

“I remember *everything.*”

“OK,” said Mandy.

She hoped that was the truth.

The Big Bag looked bigger than ever.

There were so many rows.

There were so many signs.

There was so much food.

STOCK UP SALE
VEGETABLES FRUITS
SPECIAL
PERSONALIZED Mugs

They decided to start
with the row that said SNACKS.
"Was popcorn on the list?"
asked Mimi.

"I thought you remembered
everything," said Mandy.
"Well, I *think* it was on the list,"
said Mimi.
And she put popcorn in the cart.
Popcorn was her favorite snack.

"What came after popcorn?"
asked Mandy.
Mimi looked at a row of sodas.
"If orange soda was not on the list,
it should have been,"
she said.
So Mandy put two orange sodas
in the cart.

"Hey! What about that new cereal
with the free airplane inside?"
asked Mimi.
"Yeah," said Mandy.
"Grown-ups like it when you try
something new."
So Mimi put a box of Super Krunchy
in the cart.

Soon, the cart was filled with

popcorn,

orange soda,

cereal,

peanut butter plain,

peanut butter crunchy,

chocolate ice cream,

paper cups,

tooth brushes, and

grape bubble gum.

PEANUT BUTTER
Crunchy
100% Peanuts

CHOCOLATE
DONNA PAUL'S
ICE CREAM

grape

Mandy and Mimi got in line
for the check-out counter.
They looked at the cart.
It was loaded to the very top.
They looked at the five dollar bill.

Then they looked at each other.
"We needed the list," said Mandy.
"I usually remember better,"
said Mimi.

"We'll never get to go shopping again
if we come back
with all this stuff!" cried Mandy.
"What do we do now?"
"Dump it," said Mimi.

“Dump it?” asked Mandy.

“Like this,” said Mimi.

Quickly, Mimi pushed the cart

to the back of the store—

and left it there.

They ran for the door
that said OUT.
And there was Maxi
with a yellow something
in his mouth.
"The list!" cried Mandy.
"Here Maxi," said Mimi.
Maxi chewed the paper.
"Nice Maxi," said Mimi.
Maxi still chewed the paper.
Mimi took a dog treat
out of her pocket.

Maxi dropped the paper.
Now the yellow list was
wet and slimy, sticky and dirty.
It had holes in it—
little dog-tooth holes.

"You dropped it," said Mimi.
"You pick it up."
"Yuck," said Mandy.

CHAPTER FOUR

M and M went back into

The Big Bag with the list.

The list was smelly.

And it ripped

when Mandy tried to smooth it out.

Mandy and Mimi looked

at the first word and laughed.

It said

1 butt

"Butter!" said Mandy.

And they ran to get one butter.

The next word on the list
started with a dog-tooth hole.
Then came the letters r e a d.
But that did not fool them!
They knew the word was BREAD.

apples was the only whole word.
They picked out two good ones.
The next word on the list
was *trash*.
"This is a store, not a dump!"
said Mandy.
Then they raced the cart
to trash bags.

The last word was all rubbed out.
But Mandy and Mimi knew
the word was not popcorn
or orange soda.
They knew the word was milk.
And they picked out the coldest one.
"Well that's it," said M and M.

The clerk at the check-out counter
rang up each thing.
"That comes to four dollars
and three cents," he said.

Mimi gave the clerk the five dollar bill.
He gave her back ninety-seven cents.
“Come again,” said the clerk.
“Oh, we will!” they answered.

They ran outside and untied Maxi.
Then they gave him the list.
"It's all yours now," said Mandy.
And Maxi chewed the list right up!

Then M and M took turns carrying
one butter, one bread, two apples,
trash bags, and one milk
home without stopping!

PAT ROSS grew up in Chestertown, Maryland, and came to New York City after graduating from Hood College. She is now an editor of books for young readers and has also written eight books for children. She lives in a big apartment house in New York with her husband and their daughter Erica.

MARYLIN HAFNER was born in Brooklyn, New York. She studied art at Pratt Institute and the School of Visual Arts and has made the pictures for more than thirty books for children. She is also a sculptor and a printmaker and loves to cook, travel, and collect antiques. She is the mother of three grown-up daughters—Abigail, Jennifer, and Amanda—and she now lives in Cambridge, Massachusetts.